WITH[...]

UNPLUGGED AND UNPOPULAR

AN ONI PRESS PUBLICATION

UNPLUGGED AND

ONi PRESS

AN ONI PRESS PUBLICATION

UNPOPULAR

WRITTEN BY
MAT HEAGERTY

ILLUSTRATED BY
TINTIN PANTOJA

COLORED BY
MIKE AMANTE

LETTERED BY
HASSAN OTSMANE-ELHAOU

COVER ILLUSTRATED BY
TINTIN PANTOJA
WITH **MIKE AMANTE**

LOGO DESIGNED BY
RICKY DELUCCO

BOOK DESIGNED BY
ANGIE KNOWLES

EDITED BY
ROBIN HERRERA

PUBLISHED BY ONI PRESS, INC.

JOE NOZEMACK founder & chief financial officer

JAMES LUCAS JONES publisher

SARAH GAYDOS editor in chief

CHARLIE CHU v.p. of creative & business development

BRAD ROOKS director of operations

MARGOT WOOD director of sales

AMBER O'NEILL special projects manager

TROY LOOK director of design & production

KATE Z. STONE senior graphic designer

SONJA SYNAK graphic designer

ANGIE KNOWLES digital prepress lead

ROBIN HERRERA senior editor

ARI YARWOOD senior editor

MICHELLE NGUYEN executive assistant

JUNG LEE logistics coordinator

ONIPRESS.COM
FACEBOOK.COM/ONIPRESS
TWITTER.COM/ONIPRESS
ONIPRESS.TUMBLR.COM
INSTAGRAM.COM/ONIPRESS

FIRST EDITION: OCTOBER 2019

HARDCOVER ISBN 978-1-62010-680-8

PAPERBACK ISBN 978-1-62010-669-3

EISBN 978-1-62010-670-9

PRINTED IN CHINA.

LIBRARY OF CONGRESS CONTROL NUMBER: 2019934120

1 2 3 4 5 6 7 8 9 10

CHAPTER ONE

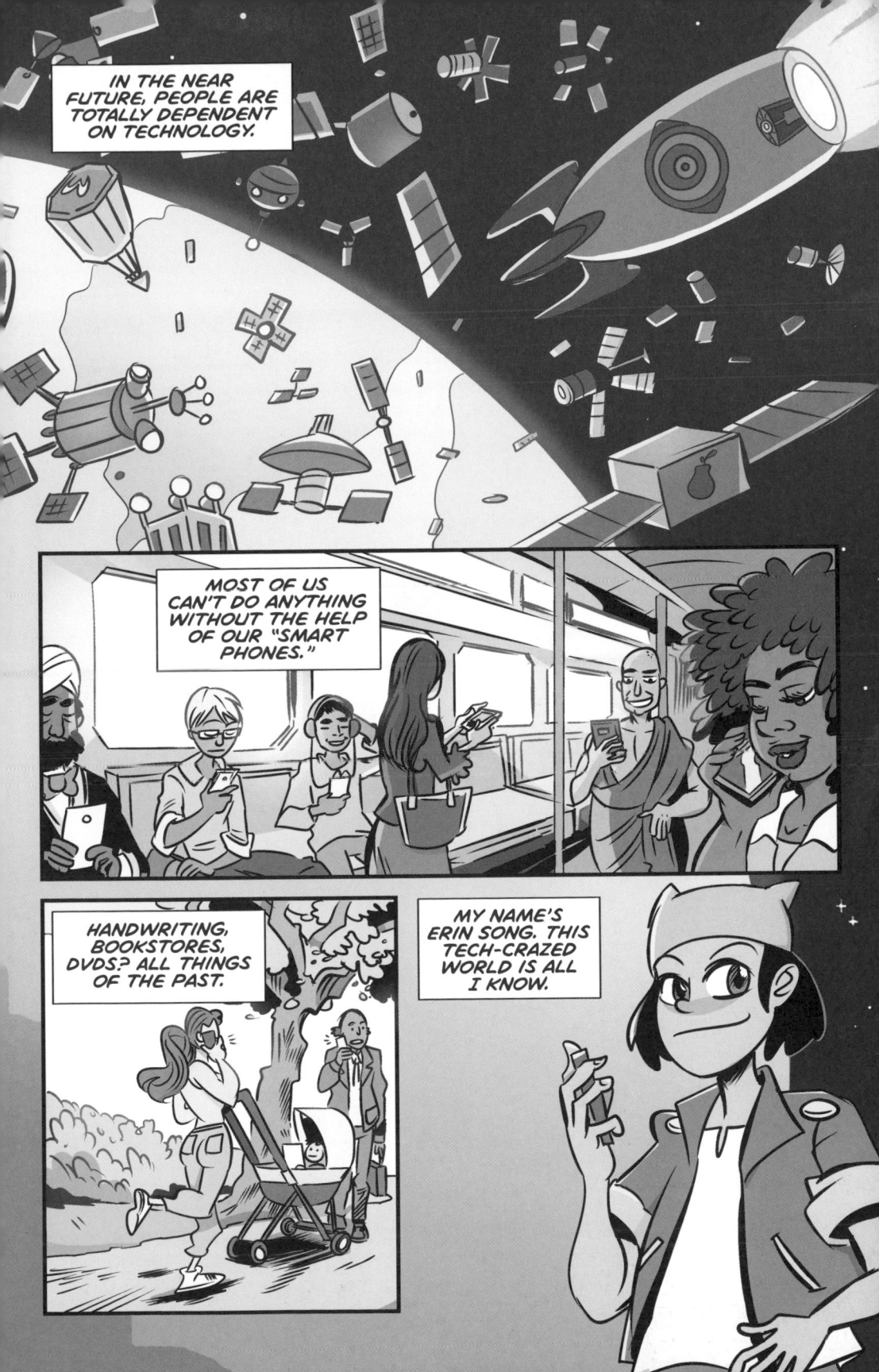

WENDY GUPTA

I LIVE ON THE EDGE OF POPULARITY. WHILE I ALWAYS GET THE E-VITE TO ANYTHING COOL, I'M CERTAINLY NOT ONE OF **WENDY GUPTA'S** "TOP FRIENDS."

7890
10526

ERIN SONG

THE POPULAR KIDS LIKE ME FINE.

1,300
2,500

I'M JUST NOT ONE OF THEM.

I WONDER WHY?

IS IT BECAUSE I'M THE SHORTEST KID IN MY GRADE?

NO RIDE FOR YOU, LI'L LADY.

HA HA!

NO, POPULARITY'S NOT DECIDED BY HEIGHT. IF IT WERE, MY PAL *CODY* WOULD BE POPULAR.

WHICH HE IS *SO NOT!*

MAYBE I'M NOT POPULAR BECAUSE I STINK AT SPORTS?

NO, THAT'S NOT IT. WENDY CAN'T EVEN DO A PULL-UP.

COME ON! JUST ONE?

MAYBE IT'S BECAUSE I'M BAD AT SCHOOL?

IT CAN'T BE. BRIAN FLYNN'S POPULAR, AND HE CAN'T EVEN TYPE HIS NAME WITHOUT SPELL-CHECK!

DUH, IS THERE A SILENT G IN IT?

POPULARITY RANKING OF GIRLS AT MY SCHOOL:

WHATEVER THE REASON, I DON'T SIT AT THE COOL LUNCH TABLE.

I SIT AT THE NEXT ONE OVER.

MAYBE ONE DAY I'LL BE UPGRADED.

THE SONG FAMILY'S HOME. CULVER CITY, CA.

MOM SAYS, "GROWN-UPS WEAR MAKEUP TO LOOK YOUNG LIKE YOU DO. YOU WON'T NEED TO WEAR ANY FOR A LONG WHILE."

THIS MORNING I FEEL EXTRA GROWN UP.

WAIT, I THOUGHT YOU AIN'T ALLOWED TO WEAR MAKEUP?

HEY, STRANGE CODY, NICE HAIR!

LOSER!

PUBLIC SCHOOL

YOU'RE A TOTAL NERD. YOU KNOW THAT, RIGHT?

IF YOU SAY SO.

SO, LIKE, WHAT'S WITH THE HAIRCUT?

NOW SHOWING

BLOOD BATH DEATH ARENA

"MY OLD MAN WOULDN'T TAKE ME TO GO SEE THIS R-RATED MOVIE.

"SO, I PUT ON HIS SUIT AND CUT MY HAIR TO LOOK BALD LIKE AN OLD GUY. THAT WAY I COULD BUY A TICKET MYSELF.

"BUT IT WAS A WASTE."

SOON

COMING SOON

JAWS 26

NO WAY, KID!

IT'S LIKE YOU AREN'T EVEN TRYING TO BE POPULAR!

YOU KNOW I DON'T CARE ABOUT THAT STUFF, ERIN.

MS. FARLEY'S MAKING US READ OUT LOUD FROM THIS BORING BOOK ABOUT SOME GOLDEN PONY-BOY.

I'M HAVING A LITTLE TROUBLE...

S-S-S-S-ENS-OR-Y

OKAY, A LOT OF TROUBLE.

PENN-PENN-PENN-SYL--

WHEN I'M NERVOUS, I STUTTER. (THAT DOESN'T HELP MY POPULARITY RANKING!)

UGH! CAN WE LIKE, P-P-PLEASE MOVE TO SOMEONE ELSE? THIS IS LIKE, P-P-PAINFUL.

SMACK!

CODY. TO THE PRINCIPAL'S OFFICE. *NOW!!*

SOMEHOW WENDY MADE HER EYE PATCH SEEM COOL...

scratched cornea

NEAT EYEPATCH, WENDY!

MAJOR COOL!

SORRY ABOUT ALL THE DETENTIONS YOU GOT.

NO BIGGIE.

MOM'S A FOOD BLOGGER, SO I ALWAYS HAVE TO TRY FUNKY NEW FOODS.
PEANUT BUTTER, MUSHROOM, TROUT BURGERS WITH BANANA-KALE FRIES!
DAD HAS A MUSIC REVIEW SITE. HE NEVER LIKES ANY NEW BANDS!
TODAY'S MUSIC IS TRASH! ALL AUTO-TUNE AND EDITING, NO SOUL!
IT'S ONLY THE THREE OF US. MY PARENTS NEVER MADE ME A SIBLING.
YOU'RE PERFECT, WHY WOULD WE NEED ANOTHER KID?
SO YOU WOULDN'T SMOTHER ME!

WE DON'T HAVE A BIG EXTENDED FAMILY, EITHER. THERE'S JUST *GRANDMA*.

SHE LIVES IN A RETIREMENT HOME A FEW MILES AWAY.

MOM ALWAYS MAKES ME VISIT GRANDMA, BUT I HATE IT! SHE'S WEIRD, SHE SMELLS BAD, AND ALL SHE WANTS TO DO IS TELL BORING STORIES.

AND HE WAS THE FIRST PRESIDENT I MET...

LATELY, ALL SHE TALKS ABOUT ARE THESE PEOPLE THAT DON'T EXIST, AND THESE ALIENS THAT ARE TAKING OVER THE PLANET.

DAD SAYS IT'S 'CAUSE FOLKS GET A BIT CLOUDY WHEN THEY'VE BEEN AROUND AS LONG AS GRANDMA.

MY VISITS ARE THE BEST PART OF GRANDMA'S WEEK. I KIND OF FEEL BAD COMING UP WITH FAKE REASONS NOT TO GO.

...THEN I HAVE, UM, THIS MATH THING, AND I'M REALLY SICK AND...

BUT I ONLY DO IT BECAUSE THE RETIREMENT HOME IS *TOTALLY* SCARY!

WHEN I WAS LITTLE, I HAD A PLAY DATE WITH WENDY. EVEN BACK THEN I KNEW IT WAS A BIG DEAL.

I MOVED MY PS6 TO THE BIG TV AND WE PLAYED WACKY GOLF.

WE WERE HAVING FUN (AS LONG AS I LET HER WIN).

BUT THEN, SUDDENLY, SHE GOT *REALLY MAD*.

DWEEB!

THEN I SAW HER WHITE PANTS WERE STAINED BROWN!

THE NEXT DAY WENDY TOLD EVERYONE IT WAS *ME* WHO POOPED MY PANTS!

I STILL GET MADE FUN OF FOR IT.

ANNOUNCEMENT

I DON'T LIKE WENDY, BUT YOU CAN'T BE IN THE POPULAR CROWD WITHOUT HER GIVING THE OKAY.

PHONES AWAY, EVERY-ONE, TIME FOR OUR MUSIC HISTORY QUIZ.

BZZZ

WENDY: Want 2 FACECHAT?

ME: In class?

class?

NDY: Put your phone in your pocket, camera out. Then hold your quiz up to it.

YIKES! SHE WANTS ME TO CHEAT?

WENDY: I know U R crazy good w/ music. I would owe U big time!

ME: Sure, no problem :)

WENDY: I knew U were cool. Thanks, E!

A NICKNAME?! I'M "E" NOW!

THIS IS SO GOOD! THIS IS MY CHANCE TO BE POPULAR!

I WONDER WHAT THEY TALK ABOUT AT THE COOL TABLE?

ENOUGH OF THAT--I NEED TO FOCUS ON HELPING WENDY CHEAT...

RECORDING ON

...AND NOT GETTING CAUGHT!

ERIN SONG

IF I GET CAUGHT I'LL BE GROUNDED FOREVER!

IT'S TRUE, SHE HELPED A CLASSMATE CHEAT!

I SHOULDN'T WORRY, THE QUIZ IS ALMOST DONE. WE'RE GOING TO GET AWAY WITH IT...

...AND THEN I'LL BE POPULAR!

TEAR!

CRACK!

WENDY. ERIN. THE HALLWAY. RIGHT NOW!

THIS IS NOT GOOD.

TCH

WE'RE SO *DISAPPOINTED* IN YOU.

WE'VE TAUGHT YOU BETTER THAN THIS!

WHAT WERE YOU THINKING?!

WHAT HAS GOTTEN INTO YOU LATELY?!

PLUS, YOU STOLE MY MAKEUP, AND WORE IT TO SCHOOL!

STOLE? THAT'S A BIT HARSH. I'D SAY BORROWED.

BIP

CODY

I heard what went down. You okay?

ERIN SONG, TODAY YOU STOLE AND CHEATED.

WE EXPECT MORE FROM...

ARE YOU LOOKING AT YOUR PHONE?!

OOPS.

I'M SORRY, I WAS JUST TEXTING CODY BACK.

THAT'S IT!

YOU'RE GROUNDED FOR **ONE MONTH!**

Grandma mooches breakfast from us on the weekends.

YOU CAN RESEARCH YOUR PAPER AT THE *LIBRARY.*

YANK!

YOU KNOW ERIN, I CAN HELP WITH YOUR PAPER.

US GEEZERS KNOW A LOT ABOUT HISTORY!

OHH, NO THAT'S OKAY...

IT'S ON LIKE... *RECENT* HISTORY. STUFF YOU DON'T KNOW ANYTHING ABOUT.

I'LL JUST GO TO THE LIBRARY.

EAT UP, GRANDMA, WE'VE GOT A BUSY DAY HERE.

"WE HAVE TO GET YOU BACK TO THE RETIREMENT HOME SOON."

I'VE REACHED FOR MY PHONE AT LEAST SEVEN TIMES.

Sizzle

I KEEP SEEING THINGS I WANT TO TEXT CODY.

UGH! ALMOST THERE.

HE MUST THINK I'M DEAD; THIS IS THE LONGEST WE'VE GONE WITHOUT TEXTING SINCE I WAS SIX.

DOING A SCHOOL PAPER SHOULDN'T BE THIS HARD. IT SHOULD JUST BE A MATTER OF OPENING A LAPTOP!

CULVER CITY PUBLIC LIBRARY

Caffeine Kiss

WAIT, WHAT... IS... THAT?

DO YOU GUYS HONESTLY NOT SEE IT?!

IT'S AS IF THE MONSTER'S INVISIBLE TO EVERYONE BUT ME?!

heh

HELP! IT'S GOT A WEAPON!!

WHAT A FREAK! I'M TOTALLY POSTING THIS VIDEO!

WHY WON'T ANY OF YOU HELP ME!?

CHAPTER TWO

AHHHHHH!

ERIN SONG IS SUCH A *LOSER.* WHAT IS SHE DOING?

STAY AWAY FROM ME!

SLAM!

YUP, *TOTAL* LOSER.

Caffeine Kiss

HOW COME NO ONE ELSE SAW THAT CREATURE? IT WAS RIGHT IN FRONT OF THEM, AND THEY JUST LOOKED THROUGH IT!

THIS MAKES NO SENSE AT ALL.

RECORDS

SAVE WATER

MAYBE I'M HALLUCINATING FROM THE HEAT?

I NEED TO RESET!

NO, IT WAS REAL. I SAW WHATEVER IT WAS I SAW.

COULD THIS BE PART OF SOME MOVIE PROMOTION? THIS IS LOS ANGELES, AFTER ALL!

EVEN IF THAT'S THE CASE, IT'S STILL DISTURBING THAT NO ONE ELSE SAW IT!

MAYBE I'M ON PRANK'D, THAT HIDDEN CAMERA YOUTUBE SHOW?

THAT'S GOT TO BE IT! WHERE'S THE CAMERA?

ALL RIGHT, JOKE'S OVER! CAN'T FOOL ME!

PLEASE LOWER YOUR VOICE, YOUNG LADY! THIS IS A LIBRARY!

YES, DEAR, YOU NEED TO BE QUIET SO PEOPLE CAN CONCENTRATE WHILE STUDYING!

...WHAT PEOPLE?

YOU DO MAKE A POINT, I SUPPOSE.

OH, THESE? THEY'RE UMBRELLAS.

FOR YOUR SHOES.

SO YOUR SHOES DON'T GET SOGGY!

UM, OKAY?

YOU DON'T GET THE NEED, BECAUSE IT RAINS SO LITTLE HERE.

BUT TRUST ME, THIS IS A BIG, USEFUL INVENTION!

READ MY DEAR

YES, WE AREN'T SIMPLY LIBRARIANS. WE'RE ALSO *GENIUS INVENTORS!*

GENIUS, HUH?
QUITE TRUE. WE'VE INVENTED HEAPS OF USEFUL THINGS.
POKE!
LIKE OUR ULTRA-WALLET! IT ORGANIZES YOUR BILLS SO YOU NEVER HAVE TO SEARCH FOR THE RIGHT ONE!
20
50
100
THAT'S POINTLESS. EVERYONE PAYS BY CARD NOW.
LEMONADE
-NO CASH-
TOSS
YOU OBVIOUSLY DIDN'T COME HERE TO MOCK OUR LIFE'S WORK.
WHAT DID YOU COME HERE FOR?

A BOOK ON THE INDUSTRIAL REVOLUTION.

BUT MOSTLY TO HIDE FROM THAT *THING* OUTSIDE...

THAT ALIEN IS STILL OUT FRONT?

THERE SURE ARE A LOT OF THEM IN THE AREA RECENTLY!

THAT'S INTERESTING THAT YOU CAN SEE THE ALIENS TOO!

ALIEN?

OH NO, THIS IS IT. I'VE GONE INSANE!

I, I'M SORRY. I HAVE TO GO...

LOOK WHAT YOU'VE DONE, CHARLIE! YOU SCARED AWAY ANOTHER ONE!

THESE BOOKS AREN'T GOING TO READ THEMSELVES, YOU KNOW?

IT WASN'T ME, JOE!

I THINK IT WAS *YOU* WHO SCARED HER.

BECAUSE YOU'RE SO UGLY.

THEY DID SAY *ALIEN*, RIGHT?

THIS IS JUST TOO WEIRD. THIS MUST BE A PRANK.

ERIN, WHAT ARE YOU DOING BACK SO QUICKLY?

THERE'S NO WAY YOU FINISHED YOUR RESEARCH THAT FAST, YOUNG LADY.

MOM, DAD, YOU WOULDN'T BELIEVE WHAT JUST HAPPENED...

MY PARENTS MADE ME GO TO BED WAY EARLY, BECAUSE OF MY "LIE" ABOUT THE ALIEN I SAW.

IT'S *IMPOSSIBLE* TO FALL ASLEEP WITHOUT TV OR MUSIC.

ESPECIALLY WHEN I CAN'T STOP THINKING OF THAT *THING*...

I CAN'T STOP HEARING THOSE TWIN LIBRARIANS SAY "ALIEN" ON REPEAT.

WHEN I FINALLY DO FIND SLEEP, I HAVE THE MOST VIVID, LIFE-LIKE DREAM EVER...

ARE YOU FEELING ALRIGHT?

YEAH, I'M FINE. WHY?

ERIN, YOUR GRANDMA DIED FOUR YEARS AGO.

STOP MESSING WITH ME, GUYS. ARE YOU IN ON THE PRANK TOO?

SHE WAS JUST HERE YESTERDAY!

ERIN, THIS ISN'T FUNNY. KNOCK IT OFF!

CODY'S MY BEST FRIEND. HE'LL KNOW WHAT TO DO!

GEE, THANKS, CODY. I ALWAYS KNOW I CAN COUNT ON YOU.

YOU'RE DELUSIONAL. DO YOU HEAR HOW WACKO YOU SOUND?

YIKES, ERIN! YOU'RE HAVIN' A MAJOR CASE OF *INTERNET WITH-DRAWAL*.

I BLAME YOUR PARENTS. IT'S INHUMANE WHAT THEY'RE DOIN' TO YOU.

CODY, I *NEED* YOU TO BELIEVE ME.

ERIN, I WAS AT YOUR GRANDMA'S FUNERAL.

THIS IS ALL IN YOUR HEAD.

OKAY, THINGS HAVE SHIFTED FROM SUPER STRANGE, TO SCARY...

THE ONLY WAY TO PUT AN END TO THIS "GRANDMA IS DEAD" NONSENSE IS TO GO SEE HER MYSELF.

First time navigating the bus system without my cell phone.

CULVER

I CAN'T BELIEVE CODY DIDN'T BELIEVE ME.

UGH... THE LONGER I'M AWAY FROM THE INTERNET, THE MORE OF A LOSER I BECOME.

WENDY AND THE POPULAR KIDS WERE LAUGHING AT ME IN FRONT OF THE LIBRARY.

WHO CARES ABOUT THAT?

WAY BIGGER THINGS ARE HAPPENING.

CHAPTER THREE

LOCKED?!

CULVER CITY PUBLIC LIBRARY

WEIRDO OLD TWINS, ARE YOU IN THERE?! I NEED YOUR HELP!

YOUR SIGN SAYS YOU'RE OPEN FOR ANOTHER FIVE HOURS!

I CAN SEE THE LIGHTS ON! COME ON! LET ME IN!

I'M NOT AN ALIEN!

I THOUGHT YOU TWO ARE SUPPOSED TO BE GENIUSES?

NO, YOU'RE NOT AN ALIEN AT ALL.

YOU'RE THAT RUDE LITTLE GIRL.

I NEED TO KNOW *EVERYTHING* YOU KNOW.

THAT COULD TAKE QUITE SOME TIME. WE'RE VERY WELL READ--

ABOUT *THE ALIENS.* I NEED TO KNOW EVERYTHING YOU KNOW ABOUT *THE ALIENS!*

OH, YES, OF COURSE. WHERE TO BEGIN?

TO THE BEST OF OUR KNOWLEDGE, IT STARTED ABOUT A YEAR AGO.

"THESE ODD FURBALL ALIENS STARTED ABDUCTING PEOPLE RIGHT OUT IN THE OPEN."

"WE THINK FOLKS DON'T NOTICE THEM BECAUSE THE ALIENS ARE MIND CONTROLLING THEM USING TECHNOLOGY.

"THEY'RE FILLING PEOPLE'S BRAINS WITH FALSE INFORMATION BY SENDING SIGNALS THROUGH COMPUTERS, PHONES, AND TVS."

AS JOE AND I AREN'T TOO FOND OF THE DIGITAL AGE, WE'VE MANAGED TO AVOID THEIR BRAINWASHING.

THAT'S HOW I CAN SEE THEM NOW? BECAUSE MY PARENTS GROUNDED ME?

YOU MUST HAVE BEEN AWAY FROM TECHNOLOGY LONG ENOUGH FOR THEIR CONTROL TO WEAR OFF!

WE DON'T KNOW MUCH ABOUT THE ALIENS AT ALL. WE DON'T KNOW WHAT THEY'RE CALLED. WE'VE NEVER HEARD ONE SPEAK.

WE AREN'T SURE IF THIS IS HAPPENING ALL OVER THE WORLD OR JUST IN L.A.

MOST IMPORTANTLY, WE DON'T KNOW WHAT THEY'RE DOING WITH THE PEOPLE THEY ABDUCT.

I THINK MY GRANDMA WAS ABDUCTED.

WE HAVE TO WARN *EVERYONE*. WE HAVE TO GET HELP!

"TRUST ME, WE'VE TRIED.

"WE'VE ALMOST ENDED UP IN A PSYCH WARD AND IN JAIL TRYING TO WARN PEOPLE."

ALIENS ARE HERE!

ALIENS

"NO ONE LISTENS.

"THEY WON'T EVEN LOOK UP FROM THEIR PHONES.

"MAYBE IT'S BECAUSE WE'RE OLD?"

THIS IS BAD.

THERE ARE **MORE** ABDUCTIONS **ALL THE TIME!**

THEY TRIED TO GET JOE EARLIER TODAY WHILE HE WAS USING THE **TOILET!**

"LUCKILY, HE WAS ABLE TO FEND THEM OFF."

"THAT'S WHY WE TACKLED YOU WHEN YOU CAME IN. WE THOUGHT THE ALIEN WAS BACK."

YOUR PLAN TO CAPTURE AN ALIEN WAS TO COVER THEM WITH A **BED SHEET?**

WELL, IT WORKED ON **YOU!**

CHARLIE, JOE! **I ESCAPED!**

ERIN! WHAT ARE YOU DOING HERE?!

ME?! WHAT ARE *YOU* DOING HERE HUGGING THAT CREEPY TWIN?

CREEPY?! NOT AT ALL! CHARLIE'S MY BOYFRIEND.

HE HAS BEEN FOR ALMOST A YEAR. I TALK ABOUT HIM ALL THE TIME.

OH, I GUESS I WASN'T REALLY PAYING ATTENTION.

I KNOW.

SO YOU'RE ERIN? I'M SURPRISED I DIDN'T RECOGNIZE YOU! YOUR GRANDMA HAS SHOWN ME QUITE A LOT OF PICTURES.

HOW ARE YOU HERE, GRANDMA? I THOUGHT THE ALIENS GOT YOU?

OH, GOOD, YOU KNOW ABOUT THE ALIENS! THEN YOU'LL UNDERSTAND THE STORY OF MY ESCAPE...

"I WAS IN THE LUNCH HALL AT THE HOME WHEN THE UGLY-FUZZY-JERKS SNATCHED ME UP!"

WHATEVER YOU GEEZERS ARE DOING, STOP IT.

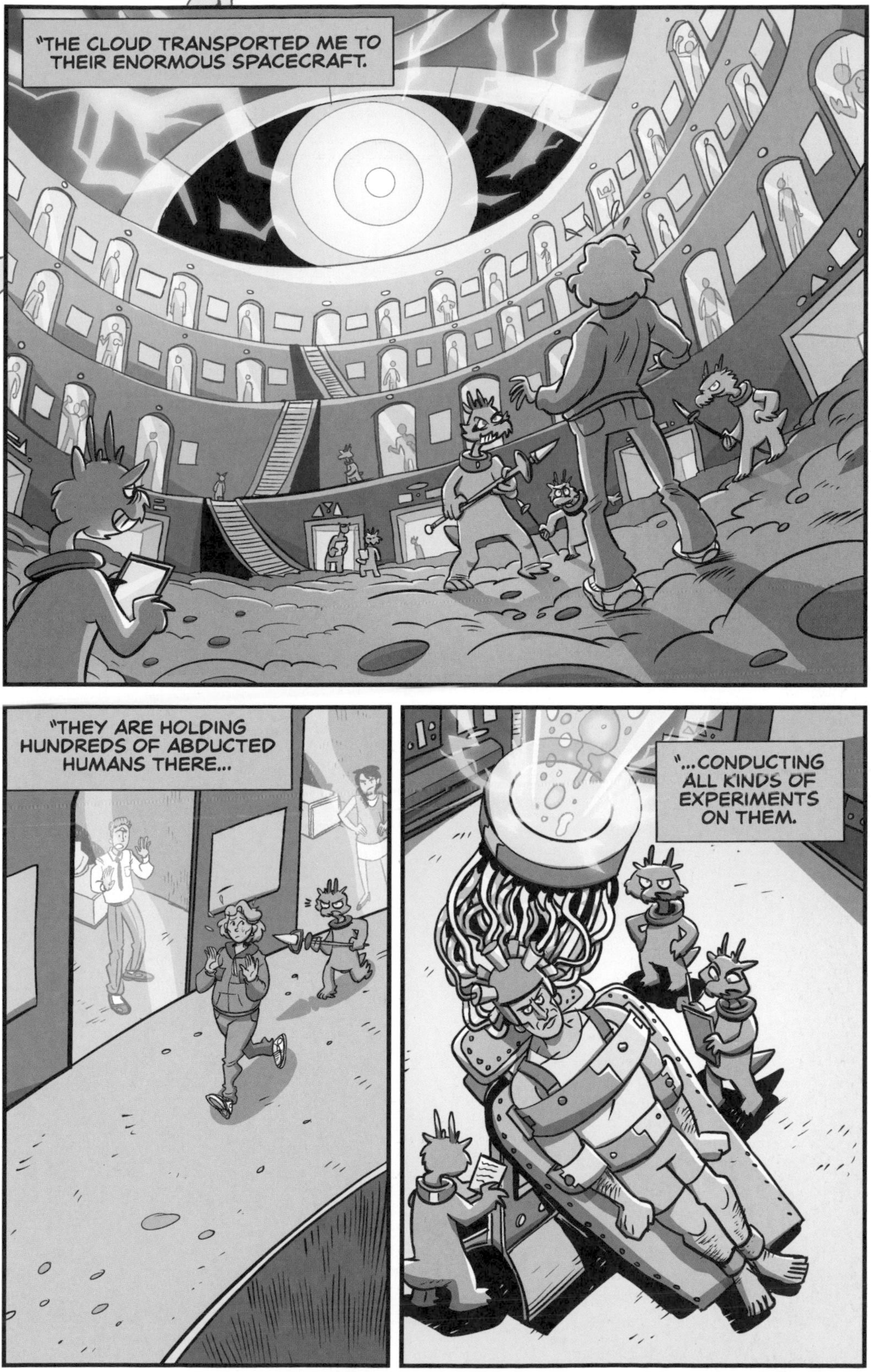

"THE CLOUD TRANSPORTED ME TO THEIR ENORMOUS SPACECRAFT.

"THEY ARE HOLDING HUNDREDS OF ABDUCTED HUMANS THERE...

"...CONDUCTING ALL KINDS OF EXPERIMENTS ON THEM.

"OVER THE THREE DAYS I WAS IMPRISONED, I WORE THE GUARDS DOWN USING ADVANCED TACTICS I LEARNED FROM *THE ART OF WAR.*"

WHAM! WHAM!

IT'S TOO COLD IN HERE, *I NEED TEA!*

TEA! TEA! TEA!

TEA!

CAN I *PLEASE* HAVE SOME TEA?!

I WANT TEA!

HERE'S YOUR DARN EARL GREY TEA! IF I GIVE IT TO YOU, YOU WILL BE QUIET, RIGHT?

OH, I'LL BE QUIET, ALL RIGHT.

WAIT, THE ALIENS CAN TALK?

YES, THEY SPEAK PERFECT ENGLISH.

NOW DON'T INTERRUPT! I'M JUST AT THE GOOD PART.

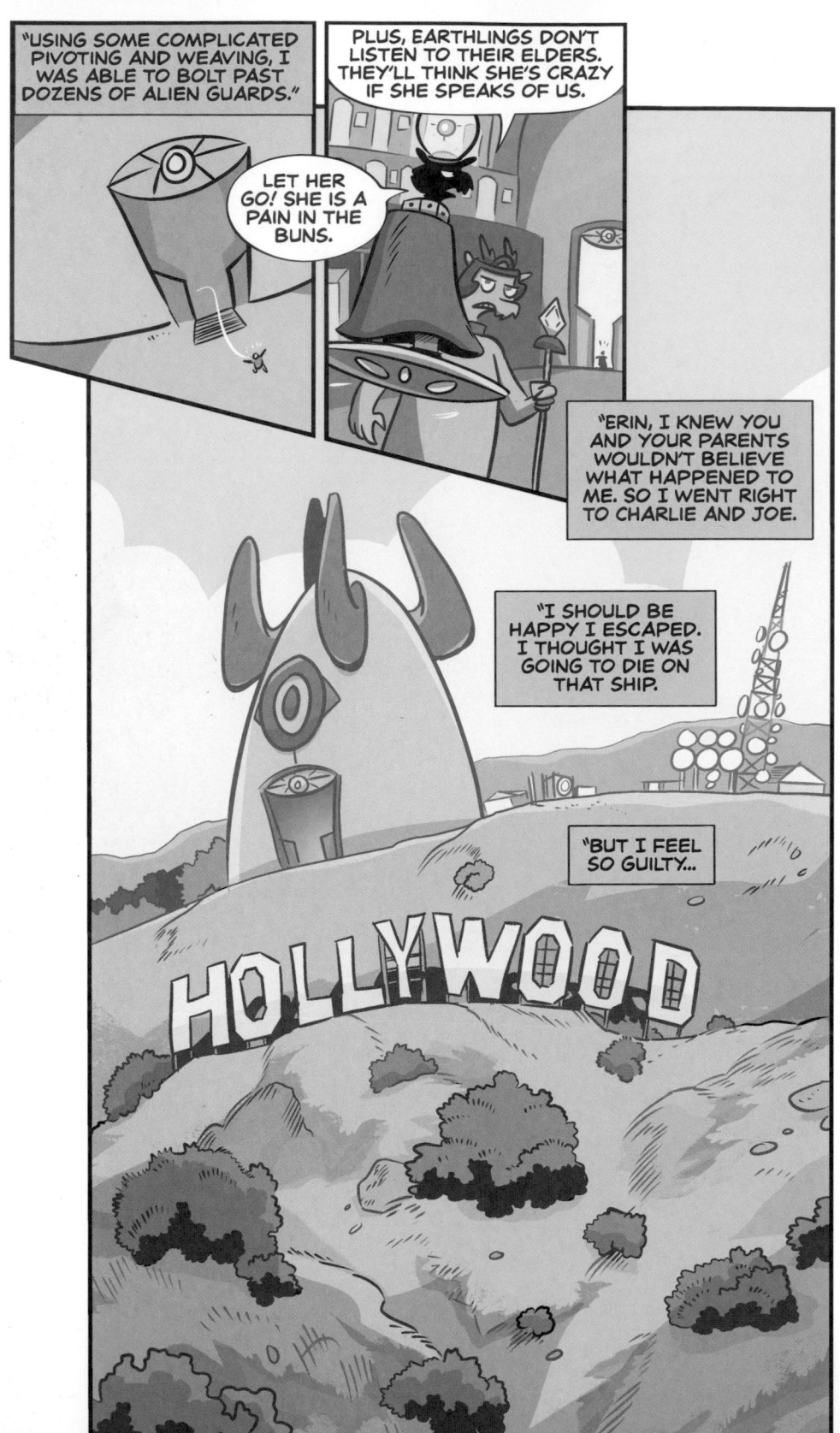

"...YOUR BROTHER OWEN WAS ON THE SHIP TOO, ERIN.

"I SHOULD HAVE TRIED TO FREE HIM.

"I'M SO SORRY. I FAILED."

OWEN?!

I DO HAVE A BROTHER.

I THINK HE WAS ABDUCTED THREE MONTHS AGO.

POOR OWEN...

WE HAVE TO SAVE OWEN. WE HAVE TO SAVE *EVERYONE!*

BUT HOW?

I'M NOT SURE YET, BUT WE *HAVE* TO THINK OF SOMETHING.

ERIN'S RIGHT. NO ONE ELSE IS GOING TO STOP THIS. IT'S UP TO US.

I'VE SEEN THEIR SHIP AND BROKEN OUT OF IT. A RESCUE IS POSSIBLE.

HOWEVER, ERIN, YOU NEED TO GO BACK TO YOUR PARENTS.

THEY'LL BE WORRIED ABOUT YOU.

MEET US HERE TOMORROW AFTER SCHOOL. WE'LL BEGIN CONSTRUCTING A RESCUE PLAN.

AND ERIN, DO NOT LOOK AT ANY SCREENS.

IF YOU DO, YOU'LL FORGET ALL OF THIS.

THE NEXT DAY AT SCHOOL IT WAS CLEAR THE ABDUCTIONS WEREN'T SLOWING DOWN ANYTIME SOON!

YOU SERIOUSLY DON'T REMEMBER WENDY GUPTA?! SHE'S THE MOST POPULAR GIRL IN SCHOOL!

NEVER HEARD OF HER.

WITH WENDY ABDUCTED, CIARA IS NOW THE NEW LEADER OF THE POPULAR GIRLS.

WHICH MEANS MY POPULARITY RANKING HAS GONE UP EVER SO SLIGHTLY.

IF I CAN STICK IT OUT THROUGH THESE ABDUCTIONS, EVENTUALLY I'LL BE THE MOST POPULAR GIRL IN SCHOOL.

OR THE ONLY GIRL IN SCHOOL...

POPULARITY SEEMS PRETTY POINTLESS WITH EVERYTHING THAT'S GOING ON.

AVOIDING COMPUTER SCREENS IN SCHOOL IS PROVING TO BE ALMOST IMPOSSIBLE.

ERIN SONG, PAY ATTENTION.

SOLUTION 1: GO TO THE NURSE'S OFFICE.

...AND, LIKE, MY EYEBALLS HURT TOO!

SOLUTION 2: FAKE PAPER EYES.

VERY FUNNY, ERIN. LET'S SEE WHAT THE PRINCIPAL THINKS OF YOUR ART!

SOLUTION 3: JUST DON'T TURN ON MY EYEPAD.

TURN IT ON *NOW* OR GO TO THE PRINCIPAL'S OFFICE.

SOLUTION 4: DESPERATION.

I KNOW, I KNOW, "GO TO THE PRINCIPAL'S OFFICE."

I HAVE TO TRY AND WARN CODY ONE LAST TIME.

THE ALIENS ARE CONTROLLING YOU WITH TECHNOLOGY!

ERIN, I'M WORRIED ABOUT YOU.

I'M WORRIED ABOUT YOU, TOO! *PLEASE.* BELIEVE ME.

I THINK YOU NEED SOME SERIOUS HELP, ERIN.

WELL, YOUR HAIRCUT IS *STUPID!*

I'M GONNA EAT OVER THERE.

I ATE LUNCH AS FAR AWAY FROM THE POPULAR TABLE AS I EVER HAVE.

I HAVE PROGRAMMING NEXT PERIOD.

THERE'S NO WAY I CAN AVOID TECHNOLOGY IN THAT CLASS.

GO!! BASKETBALL SIGN

IF I END UP IN THE PRINCIPAL OR NURSE'S OFFICE AGAIN, THEY'LL CALL MY PARENTS IN FOR SURE.

BUT I CAN'T LOOK AT THOSE SCREENS AND GO BACK TO KNOWING NOTHING ABOUT THE ABDUCTIONS.

SKIPPING SCHOOL IS MY ONLY OPTION!

I CAN'T BELIEVE I SKIPPED TO GO TO THE LIBRARY, TO HANG OUT WITH OLD PEOPLE!

CULVER CITY PUBLIC LIBRARY

BUT THEY'RE KINDA NOT HORRIBLE TO BE AROUND.

OH, GOOD, ERIN, YOU'RE HERE! WAIT UNTIL YOU SEE WHAT WE'VE DONE!

ISN'T IT TOO EARLY FOR YOUR SCHOOL DAY TO BE DONE?

UM, I COULDN'T AVOID LOOKING AT COMPUTER SCREENS, SO I SKIPPED.

THAT'S MY GIRL!

YOU AREN'T MAD?

NOT IN THE SLIGHTEST. I SKIPPED FAR MORE OFTEN, FOR FAR LESS DIRE REASONS, BACK IN MY DAY!

COME ON OUT BACK. YOU WON'T BELIEVE THIS!

READING NOOK

CHAPTER FOUR

YOU CAUGHT ONE OF THE **WEIRDOS!!!**

WHO ARE YOU CALLING A WEIRDO, *UGLY?*

WOW, THEY REALLY DO SPEAK PERFECT ENGLISH.

YEAH, AND I CAN **POOP** AND **PEE,** TOO!

HOW DID YOU CATCH IT?!

IT?

I'M NOT AN IT! MY NAME'S *GOBFREE.* SHOW SOME RESPECT!

GOBFREE HERE WAS TRYING TO ABDUCT CHARLIE WHEN YOUR GRANDMA USED THE *"BONK STICK"* TO KNOCK HIM OUT!

EAT *GLOVE,* FOOL!

THAT'S RIGHT! NOBODY MESSES WITH MY MAN!

THANK YOU, SWEETIE.

WOW, THIS ALIEN IS SO WEAK THAT, *NO OFFENSE*, GRANDMA, AN OLD LADY BEAT HIM UP?!

NO OFFENSE?

OFFENSE IS MOST CERTAINLY TAKEN!

"I'M TOUGH AS THEY COME, ERIN.

"I WAS THE *WEST COAST LEFT-HANDED ARM WRESTLING CHAMPION* FOR FIVE YEARS STRAIGHT IN THE EIGHTIES!"

REALLY?!

THAT'S COOL!

SURE, I WAS CAPTURED BY AN ELDERLY WOMAN, BUT SHE'S A *HUMAN!* YOU GUYS ARE THE STRONGEST BEINGS IN THE UNIVERSE!!

WE ARE?!

DON'T BE TOO PROUD OF YOURSELF, KID. YOU'RE ALSO THE *LEAST INTELLIGENT!*

IF WE'RE SO DUMB, WHY ARE YOU ALIEN DWEEBS ABDUCTING US?

WE WANT YOUR **WORLD**, LITTLE GIRL.

"MY PEOPLE ARE CALLED THE ONTOXITONS. WE'RE FROM THE PLANET ONTOXIT.

"OUR ONLY GOAL IS COMPLETE AND TOTAL DOMINATION OVER THE UNIVERSE.

"ONTOXITONS ARE THE POLAR OPPOSITES OF HUMANS. WE ARE THE MOST INTELLIGENT BEINGS IN EXISTENCE, YET THE WEAKEST PHYSICALLY.

"SIMPLY WITHSTANDING THE GRAVITY ON EARTH IS GRUELING FOR US.

YOU'RE NOT GOING TO GET AWAY WITH THIS, GOBFREE!

THE ONTOXITONS WILL *NEVER* TAKE OVER EARTH BY COMBINING HUMAN AND ONTOXITON DNA TO MAKE AN ARMY OF SUPER-BEINGS*!!*

GRRR

?

STRANGE KID.

MAYBE HE'S RIGHT. WE AREN'T REALLY EARTH'S GREATEST WARRIORS.

WHAT ARE WE GOING TO DO ONCE WE'RE ON THE SHIP?

GADGETS!

EXIT

SINCE THE FIRST MOMENT WE SPOTTED AN ALIEN...

...WE'VE BEEN INVENTING AN ARSENAL!

I THOUGHT I TOLD YOU TWO TO STOP WASTING OUR TIME?

OFFICER, THIS TIME THEY HAVE **PROOF** OF THE ALIENS.

IS THAT A FLASHLIGHT OR A SHOWER HEAD?

OH GOOD, YOU **CAN** SEE IT!

WELL, THIS IS AN ACTUAL **ALIEN TRANSPORTER.**

THEY'RE USING IT TO ABDUCT PEOPLE, SO THEY CAN MAKE HUMAN/ALIEN HYBRIDS--

GET OUT.

NOW.

SHOO!

POLICE

SLAM!

I REALLY THOUGHT IT WOULD WORK.

SADLY ERIN, PEOPLE DON'T TAKE US ELDERLY FOLKS SERIOUSLY.

I KNOW HOW YOU FEEL. MY PARENTS NEVER TAKE ME SERIOUSLY.

THAT'S IT!

MY PARENTS!

WE CAN GET THEM TO HELP!

THEY THINK GRANDMA DIED YEARS AGO. IF I SHOW THEM SHE'S ALIVE, THEY'LL HAVE TO HELP US.

ARE YOU SURE YOU WANT TO TRY THIS, ERIN?

OF COURSE I'M SURE!

WHY DON'T YOU TWO HEAD BACK TO THE LIBRARY AND CHECK ON GOBFREE? I THINK ERIN AND I SHOULD DO THIS ALONE.

HEY, LOOK, CODY'S BIKE IS HERE!

THIS IS PERFECT. WE CAN GET HIM TO HELP US, TOO!

MOM, DAD, CODY! *GRANDMA ISN'T DEAD!*

ERINS ROOM

ERIN, YOU'RE OKAY! WE WERE SO WORRIED ABOUT YOU.

I SAID... GRANDMA *ISN'T DEAD!*

OH, SWEETIE, WHATEVER IS HAPPENING, IT'S GOING TO BE OKAY.

THEY'RE SO DOPED FROM THE MIND CONTROL THEY CAN'T SEE ME.

GUYS, SHE'S *RIGHT THERE!* SHE'S *TALKING!* CAN'T YOU HEAR HER?

CODY, COME HERE. GIVE ME YOUR HAND.

DON'T YOU FEEL HER?

ERIN, YOUR GRANDMA'S *DEAD.*

AM NOT.

THE ONTOXITON'S MIND CONTROL IS SO STRONG THAT CODY CAN'T EVEN FEEL THAT HE'S TOUCHING GRANDMA!

ERIN, *STOP* THIS.

LET ME BY, DAD.

YOU DON'T UNDERSTAND. YOU'RE BEING *CONTROLLED* BY YOUR *PHONE!*

IS THAT WHAT THIS IS ALL ABOUT? *YOUR PHONE?*

YOU CAN HAVE YOUR PHONE BACK. YOU CAN HAVE YOUR COMPUTER BACK. *WHATEVER* YOU *WANT!*

RUN, ERIN! RUN!

ERIN SONG, YOU COME BACK HERE!!

DID YOU *SEE* THAT?

THAT FRYING PAN JUST *FLEW OFF THE SHELF* AND HIT HIM IN THE HEAD?

CHAPTER FIVE

"THESE SIMPLE EARTHLINGS POSE NO THREAT."

THEY MAY HAVE CAPTURED GOBFREE, BUT LET'S FACE IT, THAT'S NO GREAT ACCOMPLISHMENT.

ERIN SONG

VIDEO

STATS

SPY CAM 2072

SUBJECT: GOBFREE

MA'AM, THEY'VE OBTAINED GOBFREE'S TRANSPORTER, TOO. SHOULDN'T *THAT* BE CAUSE FOR CONCERN?

HUMANS ARE *LAZY, MINDLESS, COWARDLY* CREATURES.

A CHILD AND SOME ELDERS GIVE ME NO REASON FOR CONCERN.

REGARDLESS, MA'AM, WE'LL BE READY IF THEY TRY ANYTHING.

I'VE RESET GOBFREE'S TRANSPORTER TO HAVE IT LAND *OUTSIDE* OUR SHIP, AND I'VE ASSIGNED OUR BEST GUARDS TO BE READY FOR THEM.

DO WHAT YOU MUST.

HOWEVER, MARK MY WORDS: THEY POSE *NO THREAT!*

NO THREAT AT ALL.

WE'LL BE BACK SHORTLY, DEAR. WE'RE GOING TO GATHER SOME MORE SUPPLIES.

GET BACK SOON. I'M READY TO *KICK* SOME ALIEN *BUTT!*

EXIT

EXIT

EXIT

ERIN?

THIS IS TOO MUCH. I CAN'T DEAL.

I CAN BARELY GET A PASSING GRADE ON A SPELLING TEST, OR DO A SINGLE PUSH-UP. I CAN'T STOP AN ALIEN INVASION.

CODY HATES ME.

MY PARENTS THINK I'M *CRAZY*.

IT WAS SO MUCH EASIER WHEN I WAS UNAWARE.

I NEED TO FIND A CELL PHONE *NOW*.

PHONES! TABLETS! LAPTOPS! THUMBERS!

ELECTRONICS

EYEPHONE 18s!

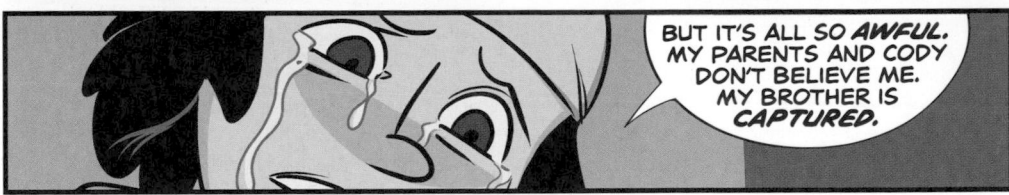

CULVER CITY PUBLIC

WHAT'S ALL THIS?

OUR ARMY!

"WHEN OUT GATHERING SUPPLIES, CHARLIE AND I DEDUCED THERE ARE AT LEAST A HALF DOZEN RETIREMENT HOMES IN CULVER CITY."

"SOME MUST BE FILLED WITH TECHNOLOGICALLY OPPOSED PEOPLE AWARE OF THE INVASION. PEOPLE WE COULD GET TO *JOIN* US!"

"THERE WEREN'T AS MANY AS WE WOULD HAVE LIKED, BUT WE MANAGED TO GET FIFTEEN EXTRA TROOPS TO HELP!"

¡¡BOOKS!!

THE TWINS FILLED US IN ON EVERYTHING. WE'RE READY TO DO *WHATEVER* IT TAKES!

THIS IS EXCELLENT NEWS!

WAIT, I THOUGHT THIS THING TOOK US *INSIDE* THE SHIP?

YOU HAVE *MORE PROBLEMS* THAN *DISTANCE*, OLD MAN.

ATTACK!

119

WHAT IN THE WORLD?

MUST BE SOME PERFORMANCE ART THING?

?

SLURRRRP!

TOSS!

BONK!

SWIPE!

THERE'S SO MANY OF THEM!

WHAT DO WE DO?

KEEP FIGHTING!

HEY! LOOK OUT!

Toss!

HA CHOO!

GOOD JOB WITH THE SPICY SNEEZE BOMBS, ERIN!
I CAN'T HAVE THEM TAKING YOUR BOYFRIEND!
MY BOYFRIEND?
EWWW!
YOU JUST SAVED JOE! NOT CHARLIE.
CHARLIE IS MUCH MORE HANDSOME!
THIS IS UNACCEPTABLE! THEY'VE BOARDED THE SHIP!

STOP THEM!

≥GULP≤ THIS ISN'T GOOD.

STEP **AWAY** FROM MY GRANDDAUGHTER!

HAVE NO FEAR, ABDUCTEES! WE'RE HERE TO FREE YOU!

YOU *AREN'T* GOING TO FREE THEM.

YOU'RE GOING TO *JOIN* THEM!

I *SODA*-ON'T THINK SO!

SLAM!

I'M NOT SURE HOW MUCH MORE FIGHT I'VE GOT LEFT IN ME!

HERE COME THE *REINFORCEMENTS!!!*

THEY ARE SIMPLY *TOO STRONG*, MA'AM! WE'RE OUTMATCHED.

MIND CONTROL AND REFRESHMENTS THIS WAY

FREEING THESE PEOPLE WILL MEAN *NOTHING* IF THESE ALIENS CONTINUE MIND-CONTROLLING *EVERYONE* IN L.A.!

REFRESHMENTS THIS WAY

WELL, THIS IS CONVENIENT.

HOT TEA!

THREE CHEERS FOR ERIN SONG AND THE OLD FOLKS!!!

LET ME DOWN, PLEASE. LET ME DOWN!

HEY GIRL, I WAS *TOTALLY* WRONG ABOUT YOU.

GET OUT OF MY WAY, WENDY.

RUDE.

WENDY JUST ISN'T COOL AT ALL. I'M NOT SURE WHY PEOPLE THINK SHE IS.

I CAN THINK OF SO MANY PEOPLE WHO ARE *WAY* COOLER THAN HER.

OWEN...?

DID THEY *HURT* YOU? ARE YOU *OKAY?*

I'M *SO SORRY!* HOW COULD WE EVER FORGET YOU?

GUYS, *CHILL!* I'M OKAY. I PROMISE.

MOM, DAD, THIS IS GRANDMA'S BOYFRIEND CHARLIE.

HE'S PRETTY **COOL**.

BOOP

HOPEFULLY, NOW THAT THE MIND-CONTROL IS OFF, PEOPLE WON'T SPEND SO MUCH TIME ONLINE.

THERE'S A WHOLE LOT OF COOL STUFF OUT THERE BEYOND THOSE GLOWING SCREENS.

HER NAME'S ERIN SONG. THAT'S HER, RIGHT THERE. *SHE'S* THE ONE WHO *SAVED* EVERYBODY.

ERIN SONG, HOW DOES IT FEEL TO SAVE THE WORLD?

UM, IT WASN'T *JUST* ME...

YOUNG LADY, YOU'RE ABOUT TO BE *VERY* FAMOUS.

...

TOP TEN REASONS TO UNPLUG!

Obviously you can't unplug all of the time—the world runs on technology. But sometimes it can be beneficial to unplug for a little bit. Here are ten reasons why.

10. IT'S GOOD FOR YOUR EYES!

Some screens, like from computers and phones, give off blue light. What is blue light? Think of the visible color spectrum as a rainbow. Colors like red, yellow, and orange have long wavelengths and low energy. Colors on the other end of the spectrum, blues and purples, have short wavelengths and high energy. Research is still ongoing about whether these higher energy lights are harmful to human eyes over longer exposure. Do your eyes ever hurt after staring at a computer or a phone for a long time? Focusing on something else for a bit could help!

9. SOME THINGS ARE BETTER IN REAL LIFE

Which would you rather see, a video of a cute tiger sitting in a tree, or an actual tiger sitting in a tree right outside of your house? Okay, bad example—the real tiger is much more dangerous. But there is a difference between seeing something on a screen and seeing it IRL. For one thing, a screen only involves two of your five senses: hearing and sight. Viewing something in real life, you can also utilize touch, taste, and smell! Okay, maybe don't lick or touch the tiger. But you get the idea: the internet is a great way to get a lot of information—just not always the best way!

8. GET USED TO DELAYED GRATIFICATION

Being online is all about instant gratification. With higher wifi speeds and tons of websites to explore, it's nearly impossible to be bored on the internet. Real life isn't the same way, though—there are definitely things in life you'll have to wait for, like checking out at the grocery store or traveling to a new destination. These things take time, and it's good to get used to not getting things in an instant.

7. SOME THINGS CAN'T BE DONE ON A SCREEN

There are great drawing programs available for artists. In fact, Tintin Pantoja, the artist of this book, drew most of it digitally, instead of using ink and paper. But there are some aspects of art that haven't been perfected digitally yet, like painting with oil paints, or creating pottery. (You still gotta use your hands for those!) There are many experiences that can't be replicated on screens, so give them a try! You might find something new to love.

6. BECOME MORE AWARE OF YOUR SURROUNDINGS

Have you ever "lost" an hour because you were so engrossed in what was on your screen that the time seemed to pass very quickly? Or, have you ever been so engrossed in what was on your screen that day turned to night without you realizing? Unplugging for a bit can refamiliarize you with your surroundings and what is happening around you.

5. GET SOME MUCH-NEEDED EXERCISE

The benefits of regular exercise are well documented. What most people might not know is that any amount of exercise is good. You don't need to be running three miles, or even one mile, or even half a mile. Walking is exercise too, after all! Find a physical activity that works with your level of physical ability.

4. PRACTICAL EXPERIENCE

Sure, a YouTube video can teach you how to make your own soap, but until you put those teachings into practice, you still won't have soap. And even with the video, you may mess up the first time... or the second... or the twelfth.... So you've got to keep at it!

3. SAVE ENERGY

If you're looking for ways to decrease your carbon footprint, unplugging is a great (and, let's face it, small) way to help. You probably already turn off lights in rooms you aren't using or shut the refrigerator door instead of standing there, gazing into it, like some kind of energy-wasting doofus. Go for the gold and unplug for a bit!

2. LET YOUR BRAIN REST FOR A BIT

Sometimes when you're on your phone or computer, looking up information or watching video after video, your brain can start to feel... overwhelmed. Of course it's great to learn, but hey, sometimes your brain doesn't like being in school all day either! That's why there's breaks at school—recess, lunch, etc. Make sure you give your brain a recess if you're spending too much time on screens.

1. MAYBE EVERYONE AROUND YOU IS ACTUALLY BEING MIND-CONTROLLED BY ALIENS AND THE ONLY WAY TO STOP THEIR INFLUENCE IS TO TURN OFF ALL SCREENS

Hey, it could happen.

X

NEED SUGGESTIONS?

The Unplugged and Unpopular team share their favorite unplugging activities below.

MAT HEAGERTY

Sweet nature walk adventures with my family, drawing rad stuff (like a surfing Pig-Dragon), going to the dog park, going to the human park, relaxing on the beach, letting my mind wander and enjoying silence

TINTIN PANTOJA

Chugging cups of gasoline-strength coffee, doodling with my fountain pens, petting one (or more) of our four dogs. If I'm unplugged, I'm probably at the country farm. There's no internet or cell signal!

MIKE AMANTE

Going on an out-of-town trip with your loved ones every once in a while, going out for a swim at the local swimming pool, playing the piano

HASSAN OTSMANE-ELHAOU

Cuddling my dog, getting lost in the countryside, eating as much food as possible, reading as many comics as possible

MAT HEAGERTY

is a chipper bartender and comic book writer who currently has multiple projects in the works. The height of his internet popularity was being retweeted once by MC Hammer. Mat lives in the Bay Area where he happily orbits around his daughter, wife, and black lab. If you haven't lost your internet privileges, you can find him on Twitter (@matheagerty) or on his website (matheagerty.com).

TINTIN PANTOJA

has previously illustrated graphic novels such as *Who Is AC?* (written by Hope Larson) and the *Manga Math Mysteries* series (by Melinda Thielbar). She enjoys journaling, fountain pens, and fine chocolates. *Unplugged and Unpopular* is her first all-digitally-inked book, which means she'd be the first one brainwashed! She also loves bad puns and window shopping. Tintin lives in Manila, Philippines with four dogs and 1/2 cat.

MIKE AMANTE

is a freelance children's book illustrator who has worked on the *Shahnameh for Kids* series and on OMF Literature books such as *Dyaran! Ang Kambal Na Hebigat! (Tada! The Heavyweight Twins!)* and *Ang Allowance Na Hindi Bitin*. He loves to drink tea, listen to lo-fi music, and read comics. He thinks aliens are cool so he made a bunch of minicomics about them. Mike currently resides in Laguna, Philippines along with his family and their overly energetic poodle.

HASSAN OTSMANE-ELHAOU

was recently diagnosed with a severe Twitter addiction. In between tweets, he has lettered comics like *Dream Daddy*, *Shanghai Red*, *Peter Cannon*, *Red Sonja*, and more. He's also the editor behind Eisner-nominated *PanelxPanel*, and the host of the *Strip Panel Naked* YouTube series. You can usually find him explaining that comics are totally a real job to his parents.

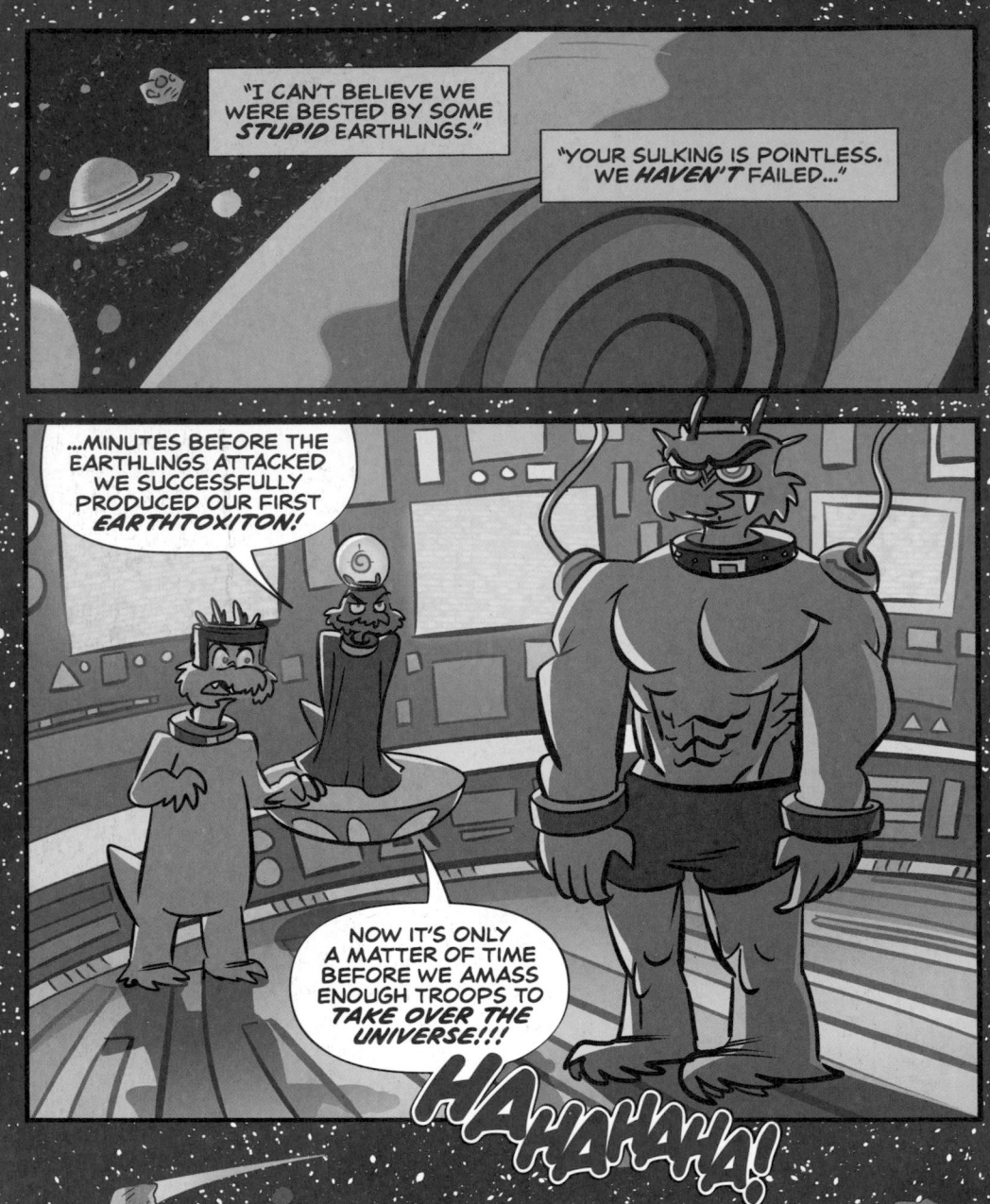

"I CAN'T BELIEVE WE WERE BESTED BY SOME *STUPID* EARTHLINGS."

"YOUR SULKING IS POINTLESS. WE *HAVEN'T* FAILED..."

...MINUTES BEFORE THE EARTHLINGS ATTACKED WE SUCCESSFULLY PRODUCED OUR FIRST *EARTHTOXITON!*

NOW IT'S ONLY A MATTER OF TIME BEFORE WE AMASS ENOUGH TROOPS TO *TAKE OVER THE UNIVERSE!!!*

HAHAHAHA!

EARTHTOXITON? *REALLY?*

I *THOUGHT* D JG BETTER?

3 1901 06207 2253

THE EN